Fairy Fay's Bad Day

Level 4B

Written by Deborah Chancellor
Illustrated by Kimberley Scott
Reading Consultant: Betty Franchi

About Phonics

Spoken English uses more than 40 speech sounds.
Each sound is called a *phoneme*. Some phonemes relate
to a single letter (d-o-g) and others to combinations
of letters (sh-ar-p). When a phoneme is written down,
it is called a *grapheme*. Teaching these sounds, matching
them to their written form, and sounding out words for
reading is the basis of phonics.

Early phonics instruction gives children the tools to sound
out, blend, and say the words without having to rely on
memory or guesswork. This instruction gives children the
confidence and ability to read unfamiliar words, helping
them progress toward independent reading.

About the Consultant

Betty Franchi is an American educator
with a Bachelor's Degree in Elementary
and Middle Education as well as a Master's
Degree in Special Education. Betty holds
a National Boards for Professional Teaching
Standards certification. Throughout her
24 years as a teacher, she has studied
and developed an expertise in Phonetic
Awareness and has implemented
phonetic strategies, teaching many
young children to read, including
students with special needs.

Reading tips

This book focuses on the $\bar{a}$ sound (made with the letters *ay* and *ey*) as in pl**ay** and th**ey**.

Tricky and/or new words in this book

Any words in bold may have unusual spellings or are new and have not yet been introduced.

> **Tricky and/or new words in this book**
>
> ## fairies behave alone
> ## wants change more

Extra ways to have fun with this book

After the readers have finished the story, ask them questions about what they have just read.

What does the Queen become under Fay's spell?
Why does Fay stop being a bad fairy?

We rabbits love to frolic and play. Can you spot us in the book?

4

A Pronunciation Guide

This grid contains the sounds used in the stories in levels 4, 5, and 6 and a guide on how to say them.

/ă/ as in pat	/ā/ as in pay	/âr/ as in care	/ä/ as in father
/b/ as in bib	/ch/ as in church	/d/ as in deed/ milled	/ĕ/ as in pet
/ē/ as in bee	/f/ as in fife/ phase/ rough	/g/ as in gag	/h/ as in hat
/hw/ as in which	/ĭ/ as in pit	/ī/ as in pie/ by	/îr/ as in pier
/j/ as in judge	/k/ as in kick/ cat/ pique	/l/ as in lid/ needle (nēd'l)	/m/ as in mom
/n/ as in no/ sudden (sŭd'n)	/ng/ as in thing	/ŏ/ as in pot	/ō/ as in toe
/ô/ as in caught/ paw/ for/ horrid/ hoarse	/oi/ as in noise	/o͝o/ as in took	/ū/ as in cute

/ou/ as in **ou**t	/p/ as in **p**o**p**	/r/ as in **r**oar	/s/ as in **s**au**c**e
/sh/ as in **sh**ip/ di**sh**	/t/ as in **t**igh**t**/ stopp**ed**	/th/ as in **th**in	/th/ as in **th**is
/ŭ/ as in c**u**t	/ûr/ as in **ur**ge/ t**er**m/ f**ir**m/ w**or**d/ h**ear**d	/v/ as in **v**al**v**e	/w/ as in **w**ith
/y/ as in **y**es	/z/ as in **z**ebra/ **x**ylem	/zh/ as in vi**s**ion/ plea**s**ure/ gara**ge**/	/ə/ as in **a**bout/ it**e**m/ ed**i**ble/ gall**o**p/ circ**u**s
/ər/ as in butt**er**			

Be careful not to add an /uh/ sound
to /s/, /t/, /p/, /c/, /h/, /r/, /m/, /d/, /g/,
/l/, /f/ and /b/. For example, say /fff/ not
/fuh/ and /sss/ not /suh/.

Fay is a bad fairy.
All day long,
she casts wicked spells.

She preys on good **fairies**.

The Fairy Queen is cross with Fay.

"Hey! This is no way to **behave**," she cries. "Just play, Fay."

Fay disobeys the Fairy Queen.
"Buzz off," Fay says.

Zap! Fay turns the
Queen into a frog.

"Yay!" says Fay. "You can
stay that way today."

The Fairy Queen hops away.

The fairies are not happy.
They stomp off with the Queen
and stay away from Fay.

Fay is **alone**.
She has no playmates now.

"Hey, perhaps being bad is not the way to have fun," she thinks.

Fay is sorry. She **wants** to **change** her ways.

Zap! Fay casts a
good spell at last.

The frog is a Queen again.
Fay chucks her wand away.

"No **more** bad spells,"
she says. "Let's just play!"

The fairies cheer.
"Hooray!" they say.
They do not stay mad at Fay.

EREADER
PHONICS

OVER **48** TITLES IN SIX LEVELS
Betty Franchi recommends...

Other titles to enjoy from Level 4

978 1 84898 771 5   978 1 84898 773 9   978 1 84898 774 6

Some titles from Level 5

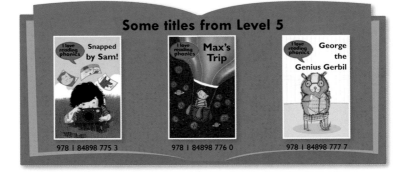

978 1 84898 775 3   978 1 84898 776 0   978 1 84898 777 7

Some titles from Level 6

978 1 84898 779 1   978 1 84898 780 7   978 1 84898 782 1

An Hachette Company
First Published in the United States by TickTock, an imprint of Octopus Publishing Group.
www.octopusbooksusa.com

Copyright © Octopus Publishing Group Ltd 2013

Distributed in the US by
Hachette Book Group USA
237 Park Avenue, New York NY 10017, USA

Distributed in Canada by
Canadian Manda Group
165 Dufferin Street, Toronto, Ontario, Canada M6K 3H6

ISBN 978 1 84898 772 2

Printed and bound in China
10 9 8 7 6 5 4 3 2

FEB 2015

$12.99